W9-AHA-802

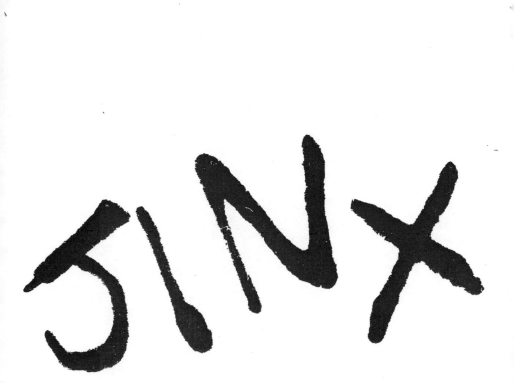

margaret wild

Walker & Company
New York

Originally published in Australia in 2001 by Allen & Unwin, 83
Alexander Street, Crows Nest, Sydney, NSW 2065; first published in the
United States of America in 2002 by Walker Publishing Company, Inc.

Published simultaneously in Canada by Fitzhenry and Whiteside,
Markham, Ontario L3R 4T8

For information about permission to reproduce selections from this book,
write to Permissions, Walker & Company, 435 Hudson Street, New York,
New York 10014

Library of Congress Cataloging-in-Publication Data

Wild, Margaret.
    Jinx / Margaret Wild.
        p. cm.
    Originally published: Sydney, NSW, Australia : Allen & Unwin,
2001.
    Summary: With the help of her understanding mother and a close
friend, Jen eventually outgrows her nickname, Jinx, and deals with the
deaths of two boys with whom she had been involved.
    ISBN 0-8027-8830-0
    [1. Self-perception—Fiction. 2. Friendship—Fiction. 3. Interpersonal
relations—Fiction.] I. Title.

PZ7.W645735 Ji 2001
[Fic]—dc21

                                                    2001056836

Visit Walker & Company's Web site at www.walkerbooks.com

Printed in the United States of America

    2   4   6   8   10   9   7   5   3   1

For my family and friends

JINX

Do not get to know me.
Do not ask me out.
Do not love me.
Be warned!
I am Jinx.

she is jen

She is Jen.
Not yet
Jinx.

She lives with her mother
and sister Grace,
in a shabby row house
in the inner west,
where babies' first words are "car" and "plane."

She loves it here,
she wouldn't live anywhere else.
But
week after week,
month after month,
each day, each night, is relentlessly the same:
school
homework
dinner
TV
more homework
bed.

She screeches at her mother and sister,
she screeches to feel alive.
She wishes for something to happen.
Anything.
Everything!

JEN >>> good girl

I
don't—
skip school
shoplift
smoke
or drink.

I
do my homework
study
hand in assignments on time.

I
look after my sister
iron my school clothes
help Mom with the dishes.

I am
sensible
reliable
responsible
(that's what my school reports say).

I am
too quiet
dull
safe
boring!
(that's what I say).

By my eighteenth birthday
I want to have
smoked (cigarettes and joints)
got drunk
had sex!!!

jen's mom will write

Jen's mom writes advertising copy.
She specializes in white goods:
washing machines, dryers, fridges,
freezers, dishwashers.
She hates these appliances
hulking
in corners,
power-hungry and fractious.
One day, she will have a wood stove,
and she'll write about things that matter—
she will write about birth and death,
about love and the absence of love,
about fathers and children,
about mothers and daughters,
about lovers and friends.
She'll write about the whole goddamn
wonderful, awful business
of loving and being loved.

jen wants to paint

Art is her best subject,
but she doesn't know
if she has the talent or the will
to be a painter.

Anyway, these days
all she wants to paint
is distant hazy scenes—
miniature houses, rooftops, pylons,
trees, spires, cranes.
Like faraway lights,
they seem infinitely more
mysterious and magical
than the hard-edged clutter of
front yards, cars, chimney pots,
telephone poles, and trash cans.

JEN >>> spiders

Mom has had two husbands:
my father (the Rat),
who ran away when Grace was born
imperfect,
and a nice-enough guy called Phil
who didn't last long.
I guess my mother was just lonely.

We have a joke in our family.
It goes like this:

Grace sometimes mixes up words,
calling huntsman spiders "husbands."
So when there's a spider in the house,
Grace and I yell,
"Quick! Get Mom—
she's good at getting rid of husbands!"

Mom laughs.
She says she's quite happy
husbandless.

But she looks wistful
when she puts on her jacket
and goes for a walk to the bay.

the rat long ago

A long, long time ago,
Jen's father rages,
How can you *knowingly*
bring a handicapped child
into the world?
One day she will cry out,
"I wish I was like everyone else!"
What will you tell her then?

Beside him, his wife lies quietly,
resolved.
He wants to punch the wall,
kick in the door.
Instead, he packs a suitcase
and vanishes for a long, long time,
traveling roads tiger-striped with shadows.

best friends

The girls are friends at elementary school,
then high school.

Everyone except Ruthless
falls out with Serena now and again.
Jen and Connie can't stand it
when Serena sulks,
but Ruthless stays out
of all the bitching,
her kind eyes noting everything,
but refusing to judge.

white lies

During Ruth's first year of high school,
a student,
stung by her refusal
to tell a white lie,
exclaimed:
"Jeez! You're ruthlessly honest, Ruth!"
From then on
everyone called her Ruthless,
although apart from her
insistence on the truth,
she is the least ruthless person
in the world.

marry me off

Connie says,
"They'll try to marry me off
to some old Greek guy.
My father will kill me
if he finds out I'm gay.
I'll tell them
as soon as I've finished school.
If they hit me
I'll scream,
yell for the police.
I'll walk out,
never see them again.
But they'll see *me*—
on TV, dancing in the Mardi Gras,
waggling my tits!"

Connie laughs
so loudly
teachers in the staff room
click their tongues.

Connie adores her mom and dad.
She won't want to hurt them.
She'll probably end up marrying
someone they've picked out,
and then what?

hard to breathe

Serena is cool,
one of the girls who smokes
behind the bleachers.
She moans about school,
the teachers,
endless assignments.
She says she can't wait
to leave,
but when she thinks
about what will happen then,
she finds it hard
to breathe.

hair

The night before a beach party,
Jen and Serena and Ruthless wax
their legs and bikini lines.

They're laughing,
full of bravado
until they start to yank off
the hair,
strip by strip.

Jen's mother gives them
two Tylenol each so they can sleep.
She doesn't say "I told you,"
and for this they are weepily grateful.

In the morning
they preen
in their high-cut swimsuits,
their legs as smooth and pale
as polished wood.

They are embarrassed for Connie,
whose pubic hair sticks out
from her swimsuit like a welcome mat,
but they're also envious
because she simply doesn't care.

JEN >>> good time charlie

I meet Charlie
At my 10th grade dance.
He gate-crashes, dressed as a girl.
Connie falls in love,
the headmaster dances with him twice,
looking entranced.
Charlie is the most beautiful girl
in the room.

Later, a group of us go to Mike's
for an all-night party.
Charlie comes too,
takes off the wig,
scrubs off the makeup,
borrows jeans and a shirt.
He's the handsomest boy in the room.
Connie punches his arm—
"I preferred you as a girl!"

Charlie asks me to dance.
I tell him he should be an actor.
He laughs, shrugs,
maybe.
His parents want him
to be a doctor or a lawyer,
the usual middle-class things.
He just wants to have a good time.

With me, I hope!

grace

Mongol:
Genghis Khan word
stocking-over-face word
brutal
but vivid.

Down's syndrome:
mouthful
vaguely medical
bland
but kinder.

JEN >>> santa's knee

Charlie lines up with Grace
to see Santa.
It doesn't seem to bother him
everyone else is only knee-high.
Grace beams on Santa's lap,
her arms around his neck.
She makes her wish,
then insists it's Charlie's turn.
I'm so embarrassed for Charlie
I could kill Grace.
But he just plonks himself
on Santa's knee
and makes a wish,
as if it's the most natural thing
in the world.

I just might fall in love with this guy.

shipwrecked

Serena's parents are as remote
as islands.
Serena feels shipwrecked,
even if it is in comfort:
TV, video, stereo, whirlpool bath, microwave.
She calls her computer Man Friday,
and when she and Man are alone
in the house,
she surfs the Net,
pretending to be someone else,
someone who is not sending out
signals of distress.

sea spray and fossils

Serena can't believe
that Charlie wants to go out
with Jen.

When they're all at the beach,
Serena splashes Charlie,
trickles sand on his back,
flicks him with her towel.

She can tell Jen is furious,
but she's beyond caring.
She only stops when Ruthless
insists on the two of them going
for a walk to the rocks.

With waves exploding around them
like grenades,
Serena bursts into tears.
Silently, Ruthless hugs her.
When Serena is sodden with tears
and sea spray,
she's able to laugh at herself a little,
and she and Ruthless
chatter about the rocks,
exclaiming over fish fossils
millions of years old.

JEN >>> strange but beautiful

The Etruscans:
mysterious
ancient people
who vanished.
They offered to the gods
otherworldly statues
much taller than
ordinary folk
so the gods would notice them.

On my desk
I have a small bronze replica:
long arms
long legs
long body
thin as my finger.
It looks as if it's been
stretched on a rack.
Strange
but beautiful.

ruthless's family

Ruthless and her mom and dad
live in a rambling old house
that has managed to withstand
the ravages
of termites and dry rot.
In the hallway,
the three of them have stripped off
layers of wallpaper,
revealing a surface
of bleached blue.
It's the color of the sea at dusk,
dissected
by a line of rising damp.
Although their friends think
they're eccentric,
Ruthless's parents like the plainness
of these bare, discolored walls.

Jen would like to paint this family,
right there, against the unadorned.

JEN >>> the smartest person

Grace can read and write.
She takes her homework
very seriously.
She borrows my history textbook
determined to read it
from cover to cover.
She can't get beyond
the first paragraph.

"I am stupid!
I am a veggie!"

She wants to be like other teenagers:
experimenting
learning
growing up
understanding
more.

"In some ways," Mom tells her,
"you are the smartest person I know,
and the most loving."

"Hear, hear," I say,
and I mean it.

Grace sniffs,
then smiles
and gives me back my book.

She puts on her favorite video.
She has watched *The Sound of Music*
more than five hundred times,
but she still loves it.

Mom and I know it backward,
every bloody song, every bloody word.
We want to strangle Julie Andrews.

JEN >>> dream machine

Charlie loves two things:
me!
and his dream machine.
It was a rusty old bomb
but Charlie and his dad
worked on it for a year.
It's a Mazda RX2 Capella
with a rotary engine,
lowered suspension,
tinted windows,
sports exhaust,
alloy wheels,
and a sound system with
subwoofers and an amp.

You can hear it booming
a mile away.
Mom says it's embarrassing:
"Testosterone on wheels."
Once, she needed a lift—
wore dark glasses
and huddled in the back
in case her friends saw her.

I don't tell her how we cruise
up and down Norton Street
making the coffee drinkers
cringe.

jen's dad

When he's down and out,
scraping to pay the rent,
he meets Stella,
whose creamy sofas are so soft
he sinks into them and never
wants to get up.

She buys him flowers from a frozen land:
tulips with green fleshy stalks,
red petals burning in the darkened room.

No woman has ever given him
flowers before.
He jokes to friends,
he was so touched
he cried intermittently for three days.
But really, he *is* touched.
He begins to feel he might be happy again.

JEN >>> hard and glittery

The Rat's new wife is as hard and glittery
as the gems in her jewelry box.

Grace loves the jewels.
Stella lets her play with them,
pile them on,
admire herself in the mirror.
It's something she can't do at our house.
Mom doesn't have bracelets or rings—
just a mortgage.

Once I caught Stella staring at Grace.
I knew what she was seeing:
a retarded, lumpy girl
laughably
decked out in diamonds.

I was so angry, I told Mom.
She looked at me sadly.
"How do you know what Stella sees?
Perhaps this is the way *you* truly see Grace."

JEN >>> **fat old rat**

I rage at Mom
for making me and Grace
see the Rat once a week.

Mom says,
"Don't be so hard on him, Jen.
Try to remember that when he left,
he was just a frightened boy."

I nearly wet myself laughing.
My fat old dad a frightened boy!
Yeah, sure!

JEN >>> step-ma

I hate the way Grace so easily
calls Stella "Step-ma."
I tell her to stop it,
we already have a mother.
But Grace takes no notice.
She loves the Rat.
She loves Stella.
Sometimes she makes me so mad
I want to blurt out
she's the reason the Rat left us,
but if I did,
Mom would kill me.
I would kill me.

JEN >>> so cool

It is hot, hot, hot!
So hot
deodorant sizzles
in armpits.
Charlie turns
the air-conditioning on
full blast
and we drive around
teeth chattering
until we run out of gas.

We are so cool!

what we don't like about our moms

They want to go with you when you buy clothes
  (all moms)
They're nosy (all moms)
They have hairy toes (Connie's mom especially)
They talk about sex and men's nice little bottoms
  (Serena's mom especially)
They have dorky clothes (all moms, even Serena's)
They want you to go on family holidays (all moms)
They get drunk with their friends and share
  intimate things about their children (all moms)
They are embarrassing (all moms, Ruthless's mom
  especially. In a café she once reached in her
  handbag for a cigarette and tried to light
  a tampon)
They complain in loud voices about poor service
  in shops and banks (all moms)
They get headaches from our music, but play their
  own stuff full blast (all moms)
They dance (all moms)
They try to be friends with our friends (all moms)
They're always saying "Wear a sweater" or "Take an
  umbrella" (all moms)
They're highly suspicious people (all moms)
They don't understand anything (all moms)
Horrible thought —
we might look like them one day,
we might *be* our moms!

JEN >>> about to burst

Charlie watches
The Sound of Music with Grace
from beginning to end!

She makes a big bowl of popcorn,
and the two of them take off their shoes
and snuggle up on the sofa.
It's probably all the popcorn,
but Grace looks as if she's about to burst—
she is so proud and happy.

get a life

When Jen's feeling mean
she tells her mother
to get a life.

Her mother goes to work
shops
cooks
cleans
gardens.
On Saturdays
she takes Grace swimming
or to the movies.
On Sundays she sleeps in,
does nothing if she can help it.
She has friends
but no lover.
That's what Jen means by a life.

Jen doesn't know
her mother's secret.
She doesn't know
that at forty-two it's just as terrible
to be in love with someone
who might not love you
as it is at fourteen or seventeen or twenty-one.
She doesn't know
you're never too old for such yearning,
however fruitless,
humiliating.

Never too old to cry into your pillow
at three in the morning when no one can hear.

Never too old to *want*.

jen's mom in love

Jen's mother
tosses out her dingy bras
splurges on
new underwear
new powder
new lipstick.

She haunts
the shops
the park
the bay
hoping to bump into him.
She dials his number
puts down the phone
before it rings.
She waits
and waits
and waits
for him to phone her.

She shrieks at herself,
"Stop behaving like a teenager!
Stop it! Stop it! Stop!"

But she cannot.

first love

Grace: Tell us about your first boyfriend.

Mom: I remember it was the middle of summer
when I fell in love with Kevin.
I remember I wore a hot pink swimsuit
with an enormous padded bra.
It was so big I was in danger of toppling
over.
I remember I had to sunbathe on my back.
If I lay on my stomach, my bra dented in.
I remember Kevin's eyes popping when he
saw my amazing figure.
I remember pouncing on Kevin in the pool
and kissing him passionately.
I remember insisting that he shut his eyes
because it was more romantic.
I remember Kevin got overexcited and
my mother got all agitated and called us
in for tea.
I remember Kevin never questioned why
I was as flat as an ironing board in my
school uniform and as top-heavy as Sophia
Loren in my swimsuit.
I remember thanking God for making
Kevin so thick.

The word "thick" hangs in the air.
Mom looks as if she could cut her throat.
"Thick like me?" asks Grace.

"No, thick like me," says Mom.
She puts her arms around Grace
and is instantly forgiven,
but she will find it hard to forgive herself.

charlie's pet

Charlie has a kitten
called Diesel,
bought at the market
for a couple of dollars.
It fits in the palm of his hand,
pats his face with baby paws,
sleeps on his chest.

Charlie's friends laugh.
They like big, barking dogs.
Charlie just smiles.
He carries Diesel
in the front of his shirt
as tenderly
as a father with a new baby.

JEN >>> silly old mom

Mom says,
"He's got you spellbound, Jen.
He's gorgeous,
but it's impossible
to have a serious conversation with him.
Do you have any idea what he's *really* like?"

What's she going on about?
He's fantastic, you silly old Mom!

specimens

Ruthless's father is a geologist,
and ever since she was tiny,
she has collected
rocks and minerals.
She displays her specimens
in cabinets with shallow drawers
so she can handle them easily.
It's become a joke among
Ruthless's friends
that she sees them as having
the characteristics of rocks and minerals:
Serena is an opal, fracturing and chipping easily,
Connie is a volcanic bomb,
and Jen is smoky quartz.
Ruthless sees herself as granite
(a common, coarse-grained rock),
but to her friends she is gold.

JEN >>> coffee bar

After school
we all meet at our
favorite coffee shop.
There's no table service,
in summer the sewers
in the courtyard stink,
a wobbly table leg
is propped up for months
with a hunk of dried bread—
but the coffee's cheap,
and the waiters are friendly.

When I'm there with Charlie,
I feel like a celebrity.
Everyone comes over to talk to him,
everyone except a very thin boy,
as tall as a giraffe.
"That's Hal," says Charlie.
"He's a good guy, smart,
knows who he is."

Charlie speaks so forlornly,
I look at him in surprise.
"*You're* smart, *you* know who you are."

"I wish," says Charlie.

drop him

Charlie doesn't turn up
when he's supposed to.
He forgets to return phone calls.
He keeps Jen waiting
at the town hall steps for hours.
Someone reports he jumped off
a bridge for a dare,
a rumor he smilingly refuses
to confirm or deny.
"He's selfish," say her friends.
"Unreliable."
"Crazy."
"Drop him," they advise,
"before he drops you."
Jen won't listen.
When she's with Charlie,
her whole body is flooded
with light.

rock or gemstone

Jen asks Ruthless
what sort of rock or gemstone
Charlie is.
Ruthless doesn't want to say.
Eventually she mutters,
"Pyrite—fool's gold."

Jen won't speak to Ruthless
for a week.
She borrows a book
on rocks and minerals
from the library,
and chooses magnetite
for Charlie.

CHARLIE >>> black

I dream in black.
Never color.
Why is that?

lean and hungry

There goes Jen's mother,
lean and hungry
for love.

She will not go to singles bars
or dance parties
or Parents without Partners.

She wants only one man,
and if he does not want her
she will dream of jumping
off a bridge
but, of course, she will keep
walking
walking
walking.

JEN >>> connie's dad

Now and again
Connie's dad craves
an Australian barbecue.
So Serena, Ruthless, and I
turn up to make salads,
slice onions, and cook
steaks and sausages.

"You girls are awesome!"
says Connie's dad,
his mouth full of charred meat,
as *we* tuck into his wife's
taramasalata and hommos.

We sit and talk until the evening
is soft and dark.
I'm glad of the shadows,
glad no one can see the envy
on my face,
as Connie and her dad link fingers
affectionately.

there be cars

Late on Friday nights
Charlie steals
out of the house,
and drives to a
deserted industrial estate.
There be cars—
headlights burning,
engines revving.
The idea is to race full-speed
straight toward the other driver.
He who swerves,
loses.
Charlie never loses.

flirting with strangers

On the Net
Serena is Rena,
twenty-two,
a computer analyst,
cool and sophisticated.
She flirts with strangers
who may well turn out to be
psychos or sixty.
She's not stupid enough
to make a date with any of them,
she just likes to chat
and tease.
One day she'll go back
to being Serena,
but right now
she just needs a bit of make-believe.

CHARLIE >>> god dreaming

I read somewhere
that all this—
the people, the animals,
the mountains, the rivers—
is just God dreaming.
I wish he'd wake the fuck up.

don't let the side down

Charlie goes to a private boys' school
where the assembly hall is as grand
as a cathedral,
the playing fields are the size
of a Third-World country,
and jocks
become school prefects.
The school's brochure extols
its "pastoral care,"
but what does this mean exactly?
No one really wants to hear
that you're cracking up,
they just want high academic results
and outstanding sports performance.

Don't let the side down, Charlie.
Be a man, be a man, be a man.

J E N >>> **fur**

Charlie is suspended from school—
his hair's too long.
He shaves his head
and is suspended again.
His hair grows half an inch,
he dyes it green—
the school starts talking expulsion.

I love his hair,
furred green like some exotic animal.

JEN >>> nagging

My mother reads a newspaper article:
"Teenage girls who play sports
are less likely to be sexually active."
So now she's nagging me
to play
volleyball
tennis
hockey
basketball
golf
field hockey!
"No," I say.
She lectures:
"Sex is not a recreation.
Emotions are involved.
People can get hurt."
"Is that why you don't have sex any more?"
I inquire innocently.
Grace looks up, interested.
Mom drops the subject.

Does she think I'm stupid?
Of course I know sex is serious stuff.
In spite of my mother's dirty mind,
Charlie and I are not having sex.

Yet.

JEN >>> grace's condition

Mom tells me,
"Grace's condition
was diagnosed early
in my pregnancy.
I nearly had an abortion."

We stare at each other,
appalled
at the horror
of not having Grace.

the houses are waiting

No need these days
for teenagers to have sex
in the back of cars
in parks
in alleys.
In the suburbs
the houses are empty,
both parents at work.
The houses are waiting:
warm
carpeted
with full fridges
televisions
parents' tempting double beds.
But—
mothers know
if a sheet is not tucked in just so
if a pillow is half an inch askew
if a blanket has the teeniest ripple.
Mothers will not forgive
their sons or daughters
screwing
in the parental bed.

JEN >>> not as romantic

Charlie and I
skip out of school early
and meet at the bus stop.
It's so quiet this time of day,
pigeons squat in the streets.

We go to my house,
it is empty and hushed.
I run a bath
foaming,
quickly
we take off our clothes,
hop in.

It's not as romantic
at first
as I'd supposed.
Knees poking up,
feet all over the place.
Eventually
Charlie lolls
like a king,
but I have the spout in my neck,
the plug digs
into my bottom.

Then I reach for Charlie
soap him
all over
slowly
limb by limb
lingering.
I rinse him
lovely
stroke him dry.

Wrapped up
in Mom's huge towels
we run through the house
like sheiks.

Then—

he loves me not

Outside
is a bright dinner-plate moon.
Inside
as she stacks the dishwasher
Jen's mother murmurs,
"He loves me not."
"What?"
"Nothing. It doesn't matter."

It does.
It matters so much
she wants to rush outside
and howl
across the bay
across the suburbs
until every crevice
every crack
is stopped up with her despair.

But there are her children to cherish,
a job she likes,
there is dinner with friends,
good conversations, good times,
there is music, and books,
there is dry-cleaning to collect
and shoes to heel,
there is housework to be done,
the garden to weed,

homework to supervise,
parent-teacher conferences.

There are a thousand chores
and some consolations
to get her through
the days, the weeks, the months, the years.

Jen's mother knows
she will be all right,
she just hopes the old hormones
pack it in soon
so she can regain her peace.

"He loves me not," she says wryly
as she switches on the dishwasher.
It shudders,
gives a thin scream,
then gets on with the job.

Later, she drifts on to the balcony
and checks out the moon.
Just faded old crockery.
Ah, well.

CHARLIE >>> worm

I read that in Africa
there's a worm that lodges
in people's bodies,
growing, maturing,
getting ready to emerge.

I've always known
I have something lodged in me,
something far worse than a worm,
something that twists my soul.
Perhaps it has been there
from the beginning:
growing, maturing,
getting ready to emerge.

CHARLIE >>> mask

I shave slowly,
transfixed
by my familiar, smiling
mask.
I want to rip
it off,
but I fear
what lies beneath.

CHARLIE >>> stones

I read about a woman,
someone famous,
who walked into a lake,
pockets loaded with stones.
They said she was mad.
I think she was brave.
As the water crept
over her chin, her nose,
how did she stop herself
from heaving out the stones?

blackness

Grace brings home a painting
she's done at school.
Usually her pictures are crammed
with people and animals,
the colors so bright and pure
they hurt your eyes.
This painting is black—
black sky,
black water,
tiny black figure
half-submerged,
one arm raised.
Jen studies the picture,
trying to think of something nice
to say.
"Who's that?" she asks.
Grace looks at her, surprised.
"Charlie, of course."

Grace often displays her paintings
on the fridge,
but this one she rolls up
and takes to her bedroom.

Jen's glad she won't have to look at it.
What on earth made Grace paint such a thing?

jen and charlie

As they're strolling at the bay,
arms around each other,
Charlie is unusually serious.
He says,
"If I was a boat, Jen,
I'd like to be moored to you
for life."

CHARLIE >>> to charlie

Shut the fuck up, you chattering ape!
Shut the fuck up, you grinning fool!
Who the fuck are you trying to kid?
Shut
the
fuck
up.

CHARLIE >>> crossroads

Did you know suicides
used to be buried at crossroads?
Perhaps it was to stop
sad ghosts
from finding their way home.

CHARLIE >>> voices

The batteries in my Walkman
are dead,
but it doesn't matter.
I've let the voices in.
They occupy my head.

thursday night shopping

He did it properly:
selected good, stout rope
practiced knots
then hanged himself from the banisters.

The house explodes
with light
as the family bursts in
lugging groceries
looking forward to fish and chips
bickering over what to watch on TV.

He was her boyfriend
he was their brother
he was their son
he was everyone's good friend.

Why?

JEN >>> in shock

Winters here are mild,
but I can't stop shivering.
I pile on sweaters,
wear socks to bed.
My bones feel as brittle as ice.
Mom says I'm in shock.
She rubs my hands and feet.
But I don't think I will ever feel
warm again.

JEN >>> at the funeral

His father weeps at the funeral,
his mother looks stunned.
She says again and again,
"There must be some mistake
he smiled all the time
he was always so happy!"

"Was he on drugs?"
"Was he in trouble?"
"Was there something we didn't know about?"
"Tell us, Jen, tell us! Please!"

They say they don't blame me,
of course they don't.
But they do.
I was his girlfriend
he must have talked to me
must have said something,
anything!

"Please, Jen. Please!"

But I can tell them nothing.

JEN >>> elegy

We are each given a flower to hold,
mine is a daffodil.

Charlie's uncle
speaks for the family:

"I remember him as a baby—
big, square head,
built like a linebacker.
God, he was ugly!
We loved him.

"I remember him as a small child
just bathed,
leaping in his mother's arms
slippery as a fish.
God, his face was bright!
We loved him.

"I remember him as a boy—
wearing his new soccer cleats to bed.
God, he could kick a ball!
We loved him.

"I remember him as a very young man—
showing such promise
of the good, decent adult
he would become.
God, it hurts!

We loved him.
We will always love him."

diesel

When the mourners have gone,
Charlie's brothers and sisters
fight over Diesel.
They each want the kitten.
It is special.
It was his.
Charlie's mother screams,
"Stop it, all of you! Stop it!"
The children let go of the kitten
and creep away.
When they are older
this is the memory
they will be most ashamed of.

The kitten jumps onto the sofa,
selects a cushion,
and goes to sleep.

JEN >>> the worst thing

The worst thing is
I was his girlfriend,
but still he shut me out.

beyond caring

Ruthless says,
"If he'd been in his right mind,
he wouldn't have hanged
himself in the house
for the children to see.
He must have been very sick,
beyond caring.
Oh, Jen. Jen."

JEN >>> on the back steps

Why?

I sit on the back steps
in the winter sun
with Grace.

She has made us tea.
We wrap our hands around
the comforting warmth.

Grace puts down her cup,
touches
her chest
her head.
She says, "He was alone."

The sun vanishes,
shadows lap our feet.
I think of Grace's painting
and I see Charlie in a deep lake
struggling in black water
weeds roping his ankles
as he tries to surface.

I'm sure Grace is right.
She picks up on things others don't.

I should have known
there was something wrong.
I should have made him talk to me.
It was my fault.

JEN >>> no charlie

The sun shines,
the moon gleams,
but there is no Charlie anymore.

The wind blows,
the rain falls,
but there is no Charlie anymore.

Screw the sun!
Screw the moon!
Screw the wind!
Screw the rain!

There is no Charlie ever again.

JEN >>> we don't care

I don't go to school.
I wait in the park
until Mom has left for work
then I creep back into the house
pull the quilt over my head
and try to sleep.

I fight with my mother
slam doors
scream
yell
throw things
smashing.

Grace hides in her room.
She's afraid of me.

I sneak out at night,
I meet boys at the park.
They are not my friends.
The old fig trees are as big and dark
as hills
and the wind is freezing,
but we don't care,
we can do what we like
out here
crouching in the mist.

I drink bourbon, scotch, vodka,
Bailey's, anything.
I vomit.
Some of the boys jump away
curse
jeer
but one holds my head
as I double up.
He has a kind face.
His name's Ben, I think,
but I'm too sick to think
too tired to think
I just want to sleep.

When I wake,
the ground is hard and solid,
yet in my dreams I have been falling
always falling.

with shame

She encourages her children
to respect
other people's privacy,
so it is with shame
she leafs through
her daughter's diary.

She tells herself
this is necessary
she doesn't know what's going on
in Jen's head,
this is something she has to do
so she can help.

All she finds is trivia
and one sentence:
"I hate my mother!"
She feels as if she has been bitten
in the heart.

Shuts the diary,
tells herself grimly,
"Serves me right."

JEN >>> two diaries

My mother doesn't know
I have two diaries:
one for sneaky snoopers,
one for me.

some girls say

Jen knows what some girls at school
say about her:
She's a slut.

The word is so juicily sexual—
slut
slot
slit.

She sees it scrawled everywhere:
on bus shelters
on benches
on walls
in buses
in school toilets
in trains
in telephone booths
in wet cement.

So far no one has written it
about her,
but they will, they will.
She will be washing her hands
in a public toilet,
glancing at her reflection,
and there it will be—
slashed in red lipstick
across the mirror,
across her face.

JEN >>> splitting up

Charlie's mother tells me
the family is splitting up.

"You'll think I'm crazy
but I lie awake
feeling his hands
touching me
pleading.
The children see him
under the stairs
waiting.

"They won't go up to their rooms
so we all sleep in the living room
like campers,
this is no way to live.

"My husband just lies there
listening
for the knock on the door
because Charlie has forgotten his keys.

"We've always loved this house
but we have to move
we have no choice.

"My husband will stay.
He doesn't see Charlie
doesn't feel him
touching
pleading,
and he wants to
so much!
He believes if he lives here
alone
Charlie will come to him."

phone calls

Boys
with young, hoarse voices
call for Jen
at two or three in the morning.

Jen's mother stumbles out of bed,
heart leaping.

She tells them off for phoning so late.
Most mutter "Sorry,"
but one growls obscenities,
detailing what he'd like to do to Jen.

She slams down the phone,
unplugs it,
checks that doors and windows
are locked,
looks in on Jen and Grace,
then burrows in the blankets,
unable to banish images.

In the morning
she's especially tender with Jen,
trying to make up for
that boy's ugly thoughts,
ugly desires.

talking about jen

Serena is used to being bad,
shocking her friends,
enjoying their gasps.

But Jen—Jen!—has left
her far behind.

The girls nest in Serena's bedroom,
eating chips
drinking Coke
talking about
boys
CDs
makeup
clothes,
talking about Jen.

"It's dangerous in the park at night,"
says Connie.
Serena's eyes gleam.
"She could get beaten or *raped*!"
Ruthless stares at Serena.
For once, her eyes are cold.
"Then you'd really have something
to talk about, wouldn't you?" she says.
She picks up her schoolbag
and leaves.

JEN'S MOM >>> tap, tapping

It's cold tonight—

My daughter is somewhere,
God knows where,
and I sit here at my computer,
writing about white goods.

I laugh at myself tap, tapping away,
but I want to weep.

Friends ask about Jen,
their voices tentative, careful.
They don't want to intrude,
but they are worried
I am so silent.

How do they expect me to be?
Tearing off my clothes?
Wailing?

I once heard a woman wail—
the woman who owns the corner shop.
As she turned to serve a customer,
her small daughter went missing.
We all ran into the street:
the postman,
a teenage boy,
me,
and the woman from the corner shop,

throwing her apron over her face,
wailing
wailing
wailing.

I wish I could wail like that—
full-throated,
primal.

But I just sit here tap, tapping away,
my heart clenched.

JEN >>> curse you

Lucky for Charlie
he was cremated.
For I would
stomp on his grave,
shred the flowers,
shatter the headstone,
sic the dogs onto his bones.

I curse you, Charlie,
you pathetic pile of dust.
When you offed yourself —
did you consider, just for a moment,
what it would do to us?

JEN >>> drink girl

I wake up in hospital
groggy
hair glued to my cheek
stinking of vomit.
There's a drip in my arm.
I'm wrapped up in silver foil
like a turkey ready for the oven.
I hear footsteps, someone saying,
"Are you the drunk girl's mother?"
Then she's by my side
face bleary
hair uncombed
as if she has just leaped out of bed.
Tears leak out of my eyes
I can't stop them
I feel so weak
I whimper, "I'm sorry, Mom."
She's holding my hand
stroking me
murmuring the same words
over and over
as if they were a magic spell
warding off evil,
"It's all right. Everything will be all right."
But it won't ever.
I shut my eyes
drifting
but I hear her plea,
"Jen, this has to stop."

JEN >>> sad for me

Mom has brought me clean clothes.
She stuffs my vomity ones
in a plastic bag
as slowly I dress,
my fingers shaky.

On the way home
Mom is angry.
"I had to wake Grace up,
explain,
leave her alone in the house."

Grace hates being alone.
She will have washed
and dressed
and left for school,
outwardly brave.

I start to cry again.
Mom takes her hand off
the steering wheel
and strokes my hair.
We drive home in silence.

I sleep until three
then I go to meet Grace.
She's at the school gate
with a group of friends.

They all rush at me
clumsy as puppies,
put their arms around me
hugging,
wordlessly telling me
they are sad for me.

JEN >>> potentiality

On our weekly visit,
Grace helps Stella in the garden.
I slouch inside,
trying to read,
but the Rat is annoyingly
talkative.
The things he goes on about!
Now he's rambling on about water,
about the potential to change.
I stare at him blankly.
"Water has the potential
to become ice," he says.
"It can also become steam."
"Yeah. So?"
I glare at him.
I love making him nervous.
He clears his throat.
"So things can change.
People can change."
I know what he's getting at.
Mom has obviously been shooting
her mouth off about my drinking.
I turn my eyes to ice.
Steam starts coming out of my ears.
The Rat scurries off to help with the gardening.

JEN >>> can i . . .

The Rat says,
"Jen, can I do anything?"
I shake my head,
turn away.
I don't want him to see
tears in my eyes.

JEN >>> package

A package arrives for me,
delivered to the door.
Inside is a sheaf of paper—very expensive,
a set of the best oil pastels,
and a note:
Dear Jen,
Hope
you can use these.
All my love,
Stella.
"Oooh, lucky!" says Grace.
"How nice of her," says Mom.
She hassles me to call Stella,
but it's all I can do to write
a stiff, polite little reply.
I put the paper and the oil pastels
at the back of my closet
where I can't see them.

JEN >>> charlie's car

Charlie's dad drives
Charlie's car to my place,
parks it across the street,
gives me the key.
"He would have wanted you to have it.
Take it. Please."

From my window I see
cars crawling over the bridge,
the brown-smudged horizon,
an airplane winking in the sun,
and Charlie's dream machine.
It's there when I get up,
it's there when I go to bed,
crusty with bird shit,
covered in so much black dust
that some Net nerd has scrawled
www.washme.com

Grace wants to know
may she wash it?
I shrug, if you like.
She spends all afternoon scrubbing,
does a good job
and goes to bed, grimy but happy.
I forget,
she misses Charlie, too.

JEN >>> charlie's dad

I see him in the supermarket
pushing an empty cart
crying.

People are looking at him
pointing
whispering
a child stares, astounded.

I touch him on the arm.
"It's me. Jen."

But he just keeps on
pushing the cart
from aisle to aisle
up and down
around and around
crying.

JEN >>> empty house

Charlie's mother and the children
have packed up and fled
to a condo so new and raw
no ghosts will come knocking.

Mom says,
"Don't they realize
no matter how far they run
they will have Charlie
in their heads and their hearts
forever?"

I think of Charlie's dad
alone in the empty house.
He will hear floorboards creak
and walls groan.
It's just the foundation
shifting
but he'll be wanting signs.

I soap Charlie's car
all over
slowly,
panel by panel.
I rinse it
lovely,
stroke it dry.

Although I only
have my learner's permit
I drive alone to Charlie's house.
I knock on the door
three times
but no one answers.

I leave the key and a note
in the mailbox.
I hope Charlie's dad will want
to tinker with the engine
vacuum the carpets
polish the paintwork to such a high gleam
that one day he will see his face
reflected
smiling.

JEN >>> unmooring

Unmoor my heart, Charlie.
Let me go.

about the rat

Jen: Tell me about him.

Mom: I remember he had lovely legs, and there
was a sweetness about him.
I remember his arms around me, my nose
buried in rough, warm wool.
I remember I was wearing my old dressing
gown and had sleep in my eyes when he
told me he was leaving.
I remember thinking "bastard!" He could
at least have waited until I'd washed my
face and brushed my hair.
I remember feeling relieved as I realized
I now only had two children to look after
and not three.
I remember feeling jealous when he met
Stella and guilty that I wasn't happy for
him.
I remember feeling sorry for him because
I had you and Grace, and he only visited
at weekends.

Jen: Ha! He didn't want us. He didn't love us.

Mom: Of course he did! Does.

Jen: Yeah, right.

JEN >>> boy from the park

At the bus stop
someone says, "Hi."
It's the boy from the park,
Ben,
who once held my head
as I spewed.

"When you didn't wake up
the others ran away.
I called an ambulance.
Are you all right?"

"I'm fine," I tell him.
"Just fine."

And I am
almost.
Off the juice
going to school
trying to study.

We smile.
He is very short
but he has a nice face.
I can tell he wants to ask me out.
I think I will go.

JEN >>> the peacock

Mom takes Grace and me
to the Blue Mountains for the weekend.
The guest house has an old ginger cat,
a peacock with jeweled feathers,
and a fireplace big enough
to consume forests.

On Sunday morning
as we are eating bacon and eggs
it begins to snow
so softly, so silently,
that at first we don't realize
what's happening.

Someone screams with delight
and we all rush outside,
lifting up our faces,
holding out our hands.

The cat looks puzzled,
bolts into the kitchen,
but the peacock stands
in the swirling snow,
unperturbed.

All the way home
Grace hugs her jar
of melting snow.
She talks of nothing else,
but I think of Charlie,
wishing he'd had a chance
to see the peacock
standing in the snow.

SERENA >>> guess what?

Hi, man,
Guess what—
I've got a nose ring.
It only took my parents
a week to notice.

JEN >>> betty the psychic

I bump into Charlie's dad
at the supermarket.
He's doing a big shop —
the children are coming over for dinner.
They've got over their fear
of the stairs, it seems.

Charlie's dad has been to see
a psychic called Betty
who lives in a brick bungalow
in Rockdale.
As he came in the door,
she said,
a crowd of ghosts came with him.
She described them—
Charlie's dad recognized
his mother, an aunt who died of cancer,
his cousin, Peter, who drowned,
and Charlie.

Charlie is happy now,
Betty said,
and watching over him wherever
he goes.
He's behind my left shoulder,
all the time,
says Charlie's dad,
looking so glad
that I'm glad for him, too,

though I don't believe a word
Betty the psychic says.

CHARLIE'S MOTHER >>> safe

I have Charlie,
Charlie's ashes,
safe
in a small box.
One day
when I am feeling strong,
I'll take his father and the children
out to sea,
and we'll let him go
in the waves and the wind.

JEN >>> nice and short

Serena and Connie
think Ben's nice.
He's got a nice face,
they say,
nice personality,
nice clothes.

They don't mention
that he's very short,
they think it will hurt
my feelings.
It doesn't bother me,
I just wish it didn't bother him.
It makes him crazy,
he thinks people are staring at him,
laughing.

He's always asking me about Charlie:
Was he good-looking?
Was he smart?
Did you love him?
and
Was he tall?
Was he tall?
Was he tall?

Aaaaah!

BEN >>> names

Jen thinks I'm gentle and kind.
She doesn't know
how I shake with rage,
how my head feels about to burst,
when people call me names
like Tiny and Shrimp.

when you were a teenager

Grace: Tell me about when you were a teenager.

Mom: I remember stealing my father's razor
          and shaving my legs for the very first
          time.
          I remember thinking that a big fat pimple
          was the worst thing that could happen
          to me.
          I remember staring into the mirror,
          realizing that my mother had lied and
          I would never be pretty.

Grace: You are pretty, you are!

Mom: Thank you, darling.

Grace (thoughtfully): Jen looks like you. A lot.

Jen: God!

connie in love

Connie has a girlfriend,
Megan,
who's as shy and quiet
as Connie is noisy and bouncy.
They are making plans
to live together
when they finish school,
but right now they don't dare
to embrace in public.
Connie says the Greek community
has spies everywhere.
"How will your mom and dad take it?"
asks Jen.
Connie bows her head,
her hair hiding her face.
"They will tell themselves and their friends
Megan and I are just roommates.
They will never let themselves know the truth.
They will never say they are happy for me."
"*We* are happy for you," says Ruthless.
"I wish I knew who *I* was and what *I* wanted,"
says Serena.

rock or mineral

Jen takes a chance
and asks Ruthless
what sort of rock or mineral
Ben is.
Ruthless says,
"He's a xenolith."
It sounds awful, so
Jen changes the subject.
Later she looks up the word:
"Piece of rock that is different
in origin to the igneous rock
surrounding it."
Jen doesn't know whether
to feel insulted or pleased for Ben.
She decides never to ask
that question again.

JEN >>> stella is ill

Stella is ill.
It seems this is something
that happens now and again.
The Rat tells Mom
she's in a psychiatric clinic
in Rose Bay.

Grace wants to visit her,
but Mom won't let her,
she's afraid the patients
will make Grace sad and confused.
"Jen will go then, won't you,
please, please, Jen."
I don't want to, at all,
but Grace begs and begs,
and in the end
I grumble, "Oh, all right,"
although I'll have to catch two buses.

I don't like Stella.
I always knew she was mad.
She'd have to be to marry my dad.

JEN >>> visiting

I walk fast,
afraid loonies
are going to jump out
from behind the glossy shrubs.

The grand old veranda
is crowded with people smoking.
Through the blue-gray haze
a man says, "Hey! A visitor!"

I smile at him.
He grins back—"Damn! I missed
the hydroponics class today.
What a blow!"

I laugh,
and begin to feel more easy.
Perhaps not everyone here is crazy.

But in reception
a woman is lying on the floor
like a fallen tree.
Nearby a man with staring eyes
crouches,
as if about to pounce.
And a young woman asks me,
"Do you remember what you did yesterday?"
"Do you remember what you did today?"
When I nod, she wails, "I don't!"

JEN >>> waiting

I wait in the lounge
for Stella—
cream walls, recessed lighting,
bland paintings, thick carpet,
comfortable sofas and chairs.
Holiday Inn for mad people.

The TV is on,
the sound so low you can't hear a thing,
but people stare at it anyway.

The place smells of disinfectant
and potpourri.

The man who spoke to me on the veranda
saunters in.
"I don't recommend the food here," he says.
"Last night we had something
that looked like chicken,
though it may have been an outpatient."
I laugh,
but when he starts telling me
about his two girlfriends from different planets,
I realize he may not have been joking.

It's a relief when Stella
touches me on the shoulder.
She looks very tired and speaks slowly,
but at least she knows who she is, where she is.

BEN >>> kids half my age

I'm not dumb.
I know I have a chip
on my shoulder.
But—hell!—kids half my age
are nearly as tall as me.
At the holidays my friends stack
shelves at the supermarket.
I get offered the job of elf
at the Fairy Shop!

she doesn't notice

Ben wants to appear cool.
He buys a pack of cigarettes,
and goes to the back of the garden
to practice.
The lighter
is like a flamethrower,
scorches his nose.
He's glad Jen
doesn't seem to notice
the burn,
but he wonders what else
she doesn't notice about him.

fantasies

Ben has fantasies
of being tall,
well-built,
mobbed by girls at dance parties.
But already he has the beginnings
of a little potbelly,
and he knows
he will be a round little man
women pronounce cute as a teddy bear.
He doesn't want cute.
He wants sexy!

JEN >>> lost children

I dig out the paper and oil pastels
Stella sent me,
and do a drawing of the city at night—
all blues and grays and pools of yellow light.
"It's entrancing," Stella says.
"It makes me want to be out in the world again."
She props the drawing against her bedside lamp—
"So it's the last thing I see before I go to sleep."

Later, when we're walking in the garden,
she tells me about her lost children,
three of them born too early, born dead.
She says she sometimes feels so sad
she just wants to bury her head
under a pillow
and never wake up.
I don't know what to say.
In the end, I mutter,
"I know it's not the same, but you have Grace."
She smiles. "Lovely Grace."
We both pretend we don't notice
the missing words, "And you have me."

STELLA >>> grief

Only those who have been through it
know about
the heaviness of grief.
It weighs down
arms and legs,
your whole body
until you can't summon
the strength
to lift
even a finger.

JEN >>> damage

Stella says,
"I can't stand it here.
Everyone's so damaged."

A woman called Katherine
distresses her the most.
She looks like everyone's
ideal mom,
but she shouts at her teenage son,
"Go away! I hate you!
I want my radiant daughters!"
But her radiant daughters never come,
just this sad boy.

Above us
the trees are noisy with birds
settling in for the night.
But even they can't drown out
Katherine chasing away her son,
beating him with words.

SERENA >>> guess what

Hi, man,
Guess what—
I've got a tattoo of a butterfly
on my left ankle.
I had to practically wiggle my toes at my parents
before they noticed.

JEN >>> a man is frozen

A man called Michael
is frozen,
a statue in blue jeans.
Then someone gets out
the Ping-Pong paddles
and Michael wakes.
He is fast,
zappy,
smashing the ball,
winning every point!
When the game's over,
he stands
still,
frozen again.

Stella looks away from Michael.
She says,
"I'm lucky, Jen.
I'm going to get better."
I nod.
This place makes me feel lucky, too.

JEN >>> tap on the shoulder

Stella and I
have made friends with Deidre.
She's a small, wispy girl
only a few years older than me.
When she's walking,
she'll be suddenly rooted
to the spot,
unable to move
until someone taps her on the shoulder.
Her goal is to walk
from her apartment to the shops
without stopping once.

After I've been with Deidre
my step is fast and firm
as I gladly hurry home.

JEN >>> touching

The Rat turns up.
He says, "Jen, can we talk?"
He takes me to a trendy new café,
all shiny surfaces
and pepper grinders as long as a leg.
It's nothing like the scruffy coffee shop
Charlie and I used to go to.
I think of that wobbly table
anchored by a bit of bread.
The Rat says, "I wanted to thank you
for visiting Stella.
It's making a big difference to her."
I shrug. "I'm only going because Grace
is such a nag."
The Rat: "I know. All the same."
Me: "Aren't you going to run away?
She might be rich, but she's not
exactly the perfect wife."
The Rat: "I'm done with running away.
What I did to your mother and you and Grace—
I'm sorry. Truly."
Me: "Hmmm."
The Rat touches my fingers.
I withdraw my hands,
fold them on my lap.
But I can feel the corners of my mouth
smiling.

CONNIE >>> wonderful

It must be wonderful
to fall asleep
in someone's arms.

JEN >>> i am woman

Grace gets her first period.
"I am Woman!" she tells
Ben and the Rat and Stella
and anyone who phones.
"I am Woman!" she tells
Gino next door
and Maria at the corner shop
and the Jehovah's Witnesses at the door.
"*They* won't be back!" I chortle.

Mom buys a chocolate mud cake.
We celebrate.

"Now that I am Woman," says Grace,
"can I have my ears pierced?"
Mom and I look at each other—
there's no stopping Grace!
"You have to be a much older woman for that,"
says Mom gravely.
"Before I've had a baby, or afterward?"
asks Grace, just as gravely.
Mom nearly stops breathing.
"Just kidding!" says Grace.

ben's mother

Ben's mother works in a clothing shop,
taking up hems.

Jen imagines her crouching
in a stuffy cubicle,
mouth full of pins,
trying not to breathe in
sweaty shoes and feet.
"I'm an expert on ankles,"
Ben's mother says with a grin.

She shows Jen her real work:
small tapestries of life in the suburbs.
The tiny figures are so alive
they seem about to burst their stitches.

"They're amazing," Jen says.
She thinks of her own hazy paintings,
and for the first time in a long while,
she wants to really *look*
at what is around her.

JEN >>> babies need love

Ben's mother tells me,
"My husband was killed
in a car crash when Ben was a baby.
I was devastated,
I couldn't look after Ben,
he went into foster care for a long time.

"Afterward I found out
he wouldn't eat, wouldn't play,
just lay in his crib, staring at the wall.
Babies need love to grow,
and he didn't know that I never stopped
loving him,
ever."

waiting up

She is afraid for her son
out at night in the city.
Afraid he will be
mugged
beaten
stabbed
murdered.

But she's also afraid
her anxiety will infect him.

So she smiles and says,
"Don't be too late."
Then she goes to bed
and lies in the dark
so that when Ben's key turns in the lock
he won't know she's waiting up.

JEN >>> just good friends

Ben likes holding my hand
when we're out.
I know he feels proud,
but I feel silly,
especially because we're just
good friends.

I don't pull away.
When I look at him
I see that grieving baby,
and I wish I *could* love him.

shopping

For two years now
Ben's been carrying around
a condom.
His mother finds it
when she checks his pockets
before doing the washing.
The little blue package
is creased,
damp with hope,
almost certainly perished.

She pictures him at the drug store
ears pink
dithering
buying deodorant
shaving foam
razors
cough drops
anything.

She doesn't want him
to be a father at seventeen.

So she goes shopping.

something simple

Ben's mother gazes
at the bewildering array of condoms:
silky smooth
ribbed
extra-thin
rainbow colored
glow-in-the-dark!
A girl
(can't be more than twelve, surely!)
says, "Can I help you?"
Ben's mother knows what she's thinking:
"Yuck! She's much too old and ugly
to be having sex!"
She finds herself stuttering,
"They're not for me. They're for my son."
Shrugging helplessly,
"I don't know what to choose."
With relish
the girl explains the lot.
Everyone in the shop
seems to be listening.
She buys something simple
but of excellent quality
and exits nonchalantly
as if it's quite usual
for a mother to buy condoms
for her son.
It's probably not
but she doesn't know any mothers to ask.

between his socks

Ben's mortified:
his mother buys him condoms,
tucks them neatly
in between his socks.

Why can't she just mind her own business!
Leave him alone!

Anyway
he and Jen
are not having sex,
probably never will.
She likes him as a friend,
that's all.

Mother
smother!

JEN >>> set her free

Deidre, the girl from the psychiatric clinic,
is in the middle of the pavement
outside the Town Hall.
Passersby are steering clear of her,
as if afraid they might catch something.
"Jen!" she says.
"As you can see, I'm stuck again."
Her smile is so rueful, so brave,
I wish I had magic powers
to set her free.
But all I can do is
tap her on the shoulder
and send her
on her way
today.

JEN >>> why?

I've seen the way Ruthless
looks at Ben.
She likes him,
much more than I do.
But she'd never try to steal
him away.
Besides, he's crazy
about me.
Why do people fall in love
with the wrong ones?

JEN >>> unbelievable

Ben is dead.

I don't know yet
what happened
just that he was outside a bar
with his friends
there was a fight
and

unbelievably

Ben is dead

Mom tells me this
in the middle of the night
she is trembling in her
old woolly bathrobe
there was a phone call
she says
from Ben's mother
she starts to cry
that poor woman
and poor you
Jen, I'm so sorry

she stops speaking
looks at me
her eyes big and scared
scared for me

JEN >>> reeling

I feel as if I have been hit
over the head
with a bat.

I reel.
Everything's unreal.

postmortem

They took him to the hospital
pronounced him dead
wrapped him in a white sheet
neat as a package
wheeled him on a gurney
through tunnels
to the morgue
slid him into a fridge

until his mother arrived
screaming
to identify the body.

There had to be a postmortem
of course:
tiled floor
white counters
buckets
doctors in long plastic aprons,
boots and gloves
bloody as butchers—
saw the skull
tap it with a chisel
lift out the brain
put it in a steel dish
weigh it
examine it
remove other organs—
heart, lungs, spleen

sew up the body
hose down the counters
come to a conclusion
dictate a report.

stitches

They shaved his head,
opened him up
like the lid of a can,
then sewed him together—
badly.

Ben's mother weeps
over the hacked body,
over the poor stitching.
How could the doctors
do this to her boy?

Her fingers hanker
to unpick the stitches,
to sew him up
with skill and care.

primitive

Jen uses charcoal
black and stumpy
to draw strange, childlike pictures—
people with arms, legs, coming
out of their heads—
but there's nothing childlike
about the eyes, the mouths.
Her art teacher says,
"They're primitive, strong,"
but Jen can tell
the pictures
give her the creeps.

JEN >>> i am famous

At school I am famous.
I am the girl whose boyfriends die.

My friends feel important.
They fuss over me like
hens with a chick.
But my enemies glance at me,
their eyes sly.
One whispers,
"Jinx!"

She says it to hurt,
but I like it.
It's a good name for me,
I shall have it.

Good-bye Jen.
Hello Jinx.

JINX >>> unlucky to love

I tell my family from now on
I am Jinx.
Grace doesn't know what it means,
but Mom is horrified.
"You are not a jinx!
None of this had anything
to do with you.
It's not your fault!"

Maybe not.
But I am an unlucky person to love.

I tell my teachers I am Jinx,
I will answer to no other name.
They raise their eyebrows,
shrug.
There are kids in my class with
purple hair
tattoos
nose rings
skirts hitched up to their butts.
A name change is really quite mild.

But the school counselor pursues me
across the playground,
floral skirt flying, earrings flapping,
oozing empathy,
"Talk to me. Talk to *me*!"
As if.

JINX >>> the boy

At
the
inquest
people
point
out
the
boy
who
taunted
Ben.

He
is
the
giraffe
at
the
coffee
shop!
Harry?
No,
Hal.
He
is
so
thin
I
could

snap
his
neck
with
my
finger
and
thumb.

JINX >>> accident

The boy Hal
gives his statement.
His eyes are blank,
his voice is cold.
It was an accident.
No one blames him.
But I hate him for
obviously not giving a shit
about Ben.

conclusion

Ben—
lunging
tripping
falling.

Turns out
he had a thin skull.
Died instantly
when his head hit the curb.
Just bad luck.

three words

Three words,
and now a boy is dead.

Hal wakes crying,
wishing that small sentence
unsaid:
"Watch it, Shorty!"

He sits up,
wipes his face with both hands,
but he can't so easily wipe away
the thoughts.

Three words,
and now a boy is dead.

He's walking with friends,
a boy bumps him,
he growls, "Watch it, Shorty!"
The boy blazes,
trips,
cracks his head.

Three words,
and now a boy is dead.

earth on wood

The Jewish cemetery seems barren—
few trees, no flowers.

There are two grave diggers
and a pile of soil.
Ben's mother and friends each shovel
three spadefuls onto the coffin.

Three, three, three.

Jinx feels part of an ancient ritual.
There's something real and oddly comforting
about the thud of earth on wood.

Ben lived.
Ben is buried.

Three, three, three.

JINX >>> the evil eye

I do a painting of a peacock—
tail spread,
beak open as if it's uttering
its harsh keening cry.
Over the eyelike pattern
on the feathers,
I paint in human eyes,
my eyes.

My art teacher praises the painting.
She says it's remarkable,
so alive
though she finds the eyes disturbing.

Did I know, she asks,
that the pattern on peacocks' feathers
is symbolic of the evil eye,
one of the worst forms of bad luck?

I stare at her,
widening my eyes as if in surprise.

Perhaps she suddenly remembers
my new name is Jinx
because she edges away,
doesn't bother me again.

BEN'S MOTHER >>> hearts

Hearts don't just break—
that's too easy, too quick,
like dropping a plate.

Hearts are
crushed,
hacked.
They bleed
into every organ,
until the pain
is so unbearable
you want to tear off your head.

mount vesuvius

Jinx is fortunate—
she doesn't often get pimples.
When she does,
they look like Mount Vesuvius.

Right now she's got a zit simmering
under the skin on her forehead.
It'll erupt, of course,
when she has to stand up in class
to give a paper,
or on the night of a party.

JINX >>> watch out

Grace touches the bump
on my forehead.
"What's that?" she asks.
It's just that annoying pimple,
which will probably still be there
when I'm sixty-five,
but something makes me hiss,
"It's my evil eye.
Watch out! Watch out!"

Grace backs away.
"Just a joke," I say. "Sorry."
I shouldn't frighten Grace.
I'm horrible, horrible, horrible.

BEN'S MOTHER >>> fine

The teller at the bank
asks, "How are you?"
and I reply, "Fine, thanks."
It's what you say, isn't it?
Imagine if I told the truth:
"My son is dead,
and right at this moment
I wish I were dead, too."
People don't know something
terrible has happened,
don't know you are dying inside.
Perhaps the old ways were best—
you dressed in black,
even strangers knew you were in mourning,
knew how to respond.
But these days everyone wears black.

SERENA >>> hi, man

Hi, man,
I stole fifty dollars from my mother's purse
and bought a long skirt.
It looked great in the shop,
not so great at home.
My wardrobe's full of stuff
I don't like.

JINX >>> shut up

I can't grieve for Ben,
not the way I did for Charlie.

I grow mean.
I grow cold.

At school some of the girls
bitch about me.
I fix them with my evil eye,
and they shut up.

I grow mean.
I grow cold.

JINX >>> i don't mind

Ruthless is silent and red-eyed,
I know she cries at night for Ben.
I want to say to her,
"I know you loved him. I don't mind."

I ask her to come with me
to see Ben's mother.
They talk,
look at photos.
Already they are friends.

BEN'S MOTHER >>> alone

When the funeral is over,
the flowers stop coming,
the phone stops ringing,
people stop dropping in.

I am alone, in my pajamas,
weeping.

There's a knock on the door.
It's Ruthless.

I'm touched that such a young girl
will sit with me
and listen to me reminisce and cry.

BEN'S MOTHER >>> stories

I will not make my house
into a shrine,
but I will leave his cap
on the hook in the hall,
his baseball bat leaning
against the wall.

I want to be able to say
his name,
I want others to speak
of him, too,
without embarrassment
or fear
of causing me pain.

If we share our stories,
we will
see his face,
hear his voice.
He will reside
within us
quietly.

attracting attention

After school
Serena persuades her friends
to hang out with her
at the shopping mall.
She hitches up her skirt,
puts on lipstick
and a leather jacket.
She talks and laughs louder
than anyone else.
She attracts a lot of attention,
but not her mother's—
she clacks past
engrossed
in crossing things off lists.

JINX >>> everyone's talking

At school,
at train stations,
at bus stops,
everyone's talking
about what happened.
It's easy enough to find out
where Hal lives.

One afternoon I walk to his house.
The curtains are closed,
the small front garden needs weeding.

I don't hang around for long.
I'll be back.

killer

Graffiti
is common
in the inner city—
tags marking territory.

But on the wall
of Hal's house
is scrawled the word
"KILLER."
It has been scrubbed,
painted over,
but is still visible,
like the underdrawing
of a painting.

HAL >>> **blame**

Someone out there
blames me,
hates me.

When I saw
that word
on the wall,
I felt
as if I'd been
punched
in the stomach.

I tried to stop my mother
from seeing it,
but she did.

I hate whoever
wrote on the wall.
I'll never forgive them.

JINX >>> spotlight

At night
I use the phone booth
up the road.

I make my voice rough,
"Your son is a killer!"

I hear the woman drop the phone.
A man says,
"Who are you? Why're you doing this?
My wife is ill, leave us alone."

The moon is like a spotlight.
I slither home.

JINX >>> vicious

I'm trying to study for a history exam,
but Grace is watching *The Sound of Music*
again!
Every time old Julie belts out a song,
Grace turns the sound up, up, up!
I leap across the room,
switch off the video,
fix Grace with my evil eye.
I hiss, "Don't move until I say so!"
Grace stares at me, petrified,
her mouth hanging open.
I work in peace for twenty minutes,
until Mom comes in and asks Grace
to help with dinner.
Through clenched teeth, Grace whispers,
"I can't move. Jinx's evil eye is watching me."
Mom loses it.
She screeches,
"How could you do that to Grace!
You never used to be vicious.
What's happening to you?"

Don't know.
Don't know.
Don't know.

friends

Together, Jinx and Ruthless
do a geography assignment
on soil erosion.
Jinx feels as if she is one of those
trees clinging to the hillside
as the soil creeps downward.
One day she'll just topple.
But Ruthless says,
"Not all trees tip over.
Some curve their trunks,
and grow up into the light."

dirty little secret

She doesn't tell anyone
what she's been doing to Hal.
It's her dark, dirty little secret.
Perhaps Ruthless guesses,
because she says,
"That boy Hal must be feeling very bad,
though it really wasn't his fault,
was it, Jinx, was it?"

fault line

Usually on a Saturday night
they'd all be doing something together—
going to the movies,
out for a pizza,
watching a video.
But Connie is mooning over Megan,
Serena is lost and drifting,
Jinx is set on punishment,
and Ruthless is alone with a book on
earthquakes and seismology.
It seems to her
their friendships are right on
a fault line,
and at any moment
the stresses are going to be too much,
and they will be pulled apart.

JINX >>> another world

Mom takes Grace and me
to the south coast for a few days.
We rent a house—
shabby, but right on the beach.

It's much too cold to swim,
but Grace finds a warm puddle of a rock pool.
She sits in it like a big, happy baby,
trickling sand through her fingers.

I plod along the beach,
watching the waves unraveling,
dry sand smoking in the wind.
To my right is a smudge of bushland,
behind me Black Rock.

At night the moon seems huge,
and the sky is carbon black,
punchy with stars.

It's another world out here—
it makes me feel insignificant,
small.
Small and mean.

most embarrassing moment

Jinx: What was the most embarrassing thing
that ever happened to you?

Mom: Well, you remember Great-Auntie Sara?
She loved you kids when you were
little, but I was so busy we lost touch.
Years later I found out she was very ill in
the hospital and could do with some
visitors.

Jinx: This doesn't sound promising.

Mom: Don't be impatient, it gets better.
She was covered in tubes, couldn't speak,
so I talked. For about two hours. Told her
every detail. What you kids were doing at
school, how my job was going. I went on
and on and on. It was exhausting.

Jinx: I'm still waiting.

Mom: When I got home, I had a phone call
from the hospital. Great-Auntie Sara
was wondering why I hadn't visited.
I suddenly realized I had subjected a
complete stranger to the minutiae of
my life!

Jinx: Not bad. What happened then?

Mom: I went back the next day, saw Great-
         Auntie Sara, and popped in to apologize
         to the woman. But she wasn't there.

Jinx: You probably bored her to death.

Mom (thoughtfully): I don't think so. I'm sure I saw
         her tubes twitch when I told her what
         happened to you at your school concert.

Jinx: Mom!

Grace: What happened? Tell me, tell me!

Jinx: You realize, if you tell her, you shall have
         to die.

Mom: In that case my lips are sealed.

Grace: I've got secrets, too, you know—and I'm
         not going to tell *you*, so there!

JINX >>> sturdy little thing

In the late afternoon
we walk along the beach.
The sand is scratchy
with seagull footprints,
mysterious as hieroglyphics.
Grace is very taken
with a one-legged seagull.
She worries that the others tease it,
that it can't compete for food.
But then it hops away
sturdily,
it's a tough little thing.
Grace laughs,
able now to enjoy
a yellow kite swooping
in the wind.

JINX'S MOM >>> dangers

The wind blows all the time
day and night.
The man at the general store
says sourly,
"This wind drives you mad."
There's a strange glitter in his eyes,
the shelves are stacked with horror movies.
I grab bread and milk,
don't go back.

At night
the thrum of the sea
is like a lullaby,
but then I remember
lullabies are full
of dangers and warnings.

I look in on Grace and Jinx.
Grace is snuffling softly
as she always does in her sleep,
but Jinx is still and silent.
I bend over her,
as I did when she was a baby,
just to make sure she's breathing.

jinx dreams

She dreams of Charlie.
He's in the coffee shop,
his bright head gleaming
out of charcoal blackness;
his right hand resting
on Hal's shoulder.
She cries, "Charlie!"
He turns
and looks at her,
his face pale,
accusing.
She realizes with shock
he is protecting
Hal.

declaration

A story is doing the rounds—
a woman in the accounts department
has declared
her love
to the man she works with.
Unfortunately,
he doesn't love her at all.
When Jinx's mom hears the gossip,
she feels herself flushing—
her neck, her face, even her ears,
stain red.
She locks herself in the restroom,
eyes squeezed tight,
arms crushing her body
like a straitjacket.
She's come so close,
many times,
to declaring *her* love to the man
she lunches with once a week.
Thank God she did not!

She splashes water on her face,
combs her hair,
and goes back to work.

CONNIE >>> holding

All I want
is to hold
my girl's hand
as we stroll
down the street.

JINX >>> the promise

Mom and Grace
are out at a parent-teacher conference.
The house is dark
but not empty.
A floorboard creaks,
a door swings open.
I feel cold breath on the back of my neck.
Charlie!
I long to tell him
I will never forget him, that some part of me
will always miss him, always love him.
But I know that isn't why he is here.
"I *will* find Hal," I promise.
"I will make amends."

JINX >>> searching

Jinx haunts the coffee shop,
searching for the giraffe,
the boy Hal.
At last she sees him—
he's alone, staring into space.
The place is crowded,
it's simple to jostle him,
spill her glass of water.
She braces herself for the words:
"Watch it, bitch!"
But he smiles,
says it doesn't matter,
offers to get her more water.
Suddenly they're sitting together,
talking easily,
as if they have known each other
all their lives.
She wants to get it over with,
say sorry
about the graffiti,
the phone calls.
But then he would know
how truly horrible she is,
and those sharp green eyes
would look at her with disgust.

JINX >>> haunting

We don't stay long at the coffee shop,
Hal has to collect his brothers
from after-school care.

That night I dream of Charlie again.
We are together at the beach house,
looking out of the window.
Nothing moves—
not sea or sky or sand.
Even the seagulls
are as still as stones.
It's as if the world has stopped.

"Stop haunting me," I say crossly.
"I'm going to put things right."

But how? And when?

tea for two

Late at night
Hal feels his way through
the darkened rooms.
He can hear the fridge snoring,
it's an oddly comforting sound.
That and the strip of yellow light
under the kitchen door
suddenly make him feel less alone.
His mother is at the table,
hunched over a mug of hot tea.
She smiles at him.
"I couldn't sleep either.
Want a cup?"
Hal nods.
He can't help staring.
He hasn't before seen his mom
without her wig.
Although she finds it hot and scratchy,
she wears it all the time,
so as not to frighten the little boys.
"I look ugly," she says now. "Sorry."
"You look great," Hal says.
He means it.
The shape of her skull
is astonishingly beautiful.
His mom catches his hand
and lays it against her cheek.
"I'm lucky to have your dad and you,"
she says.

flying away

When Serena was seven
she ran away—
as far as the end of the street.
She took her money box,
her tattered green rabbit,
and a peanut-butter sandwich.
This time she packs a bag,
draws out all her savings,
and leaves a map with cryptic clues
for her parents.
If they can be bothered,
they'll find out
she's flown away
to a desert island.

JINX >>> shopping

At the shopping mall
I see Hal.
He is struggling with bulgy plastic bags,
trying to keep an eye on
two little boys as jumpy as grasshoppers.
"Hi," I say.
A bag splits—
a bottle of lemonade thumps to the ground,
rolls down the walkway.
The kids scamper after the bottle,
one of them gives it a kick.
Hal groans.
I retrieve the bottle and the boys
insist on helping carry the bags
to Hal's house,
I know it's only two blocks away.
The little boys—Sam and Brian—are hugely
entertained by my name.
"Jinx," they chant. "Jinx, minx, lynx, sphinx!"
Hal grins.
He says, "Are you a sphinx, Jinx?"

JINX >>> sitting still

Hal's dad is as short and wide
as Hal is tall and thin.
He doesn't recognize my voice
from the phone calls,
but all the same I say little.
I'm asked to stay to lunch—
bread and salad.
Hal's dad says,
"We're a vegetarian household now.
My wife's had chemo,
the smell of meat makes her sick."
I sit very still,
hearing the woman gasp at midnight
at my rough, ugly words.

how to begin?

On the beach
Serena's father
takes off his socks and shoes.
His feet are as pale as fish
that dwell in the deep.
Serena's mother is showing
signs of withdrawal—
there are no faxes, phones, or E-mails
on this island.
The three of them sit in silence.
They know they have to talk,
but how to begin?
Serena digs her heels into the sand.
Away from the city
her parents seem uncertain and old.
Surprisingly, she feels a rush
of pity for them.
Gruffly, she begins to talk.

window-shopping

One Saturday morning
Connie and Megan go
window-shopping at the Supa-Center.
They look at sofas, at beds,
at wardrobes, at coffee tables.
"Bit young to be getting married, girls,
aren't you?" jokes a sales assistant.
He has wet lips
and eyes that rove boldly over Megan.
"Actually, we're *lesbians*,"
says Connie loudly.
She's so angry she doesn't care if
beady-eyed crones in black pop up
from behind every potted plant.
The man's sticking-out ears
burn red as roses.
Connie feels like plucking them.
She puts her arm around Megan's waist,
and the two of them saunter off
to look at TVs.

SERENA >>> snail mail

Hi, Ruthless,
sorry I disappeared so suddenly.
I was desperate.
My mom and dad
have been great—
they cried when they found me.
I've never seen either of them
cry.
Tell you about it soon.
Loads of love,
to Connie and Jinx, too.
P.S. I'll be back before you get this!
P.P.S. You should see the chef—
he's hot!!!

JINX >>> always

Serena and Connie
are intrigued that I'm going out
with Hal.
They think the whole thing's weird,
but Ruthless understands.
"I'm happy for you, Jinx."

I hug her,
knowing
whatever happens,
Ruthless and I will always be friends.
We will be friends at university,
friends when we're young women with children,
friends when we're successful career women
worrying about our teenage daughters,
friends when we're little old ladies
having hip operations,
meeting for lunch,
boasting about our grandchildren.
We will always be friends.

JINX >>> hal

I can't imagine
ever growing tired of Hal.
He doesn't just talk about
cars and football and bands.
He wonders—
Why do we dream?
Do animals have feelings?
Is there such a thing as evil?
Do we live the same life over and over again?
If there is a God, who created God?
I'll have to ask Ruthless
what sort of rock or mineral
she thinks he is.
I know
it will be the most interesting one in the book!

found objects

Jinx takes Hal to an exhibition
of sculptures made from found objects:
cardboard boxes, plastic containers,
scraps of cloth, splintered wood, old iron.
They walk around the sculptures,
peering at them from every angle.
It's amazing how ordinary household debris
can be transformed into something
surprising and meaningful.
Jinx particularly admires a sculpture,
layered like sedimentary rock,
revealing objects accumulated
over the course of someone's life.
It makes her think of her own life,
her own debris,
her own possibilities.

onion skins

Ruthless brings Jinx a present,
a weathered lump of rock
from her precious collection.
She shows Jinx how
several layers are peeling off
like onion skins
from the underlying, solid rock.

Without comment,
Ruthless places the rock on Jinx's desk
where she can see it and touch it.

Although Jinx hasn't been weathered
by wind and temperature and water,
she feels just as eroded.

But she will not crack apart.

JINX >>> my heart sings

Whenever I see Hal,
he always says softly,
"Hello, you."
It sounds nothing special,
but it makes my heart sing.

JINX >>> sweet simon

Grace has got a boyfriend!
Sweet Simon,
who thinks Grace is wonderful.
Grace hogs the phone,
hand on hip, exclaiming,
"Can't a person get any privacy around here!"
Mom nearly weeps with joy—
Grace sounds just like any other teenager.

Grace and Simon
hold hands,
whisper,
giggle.
Mom stops weeping with joy.
She starts worrying—about sex, of course.
Then she hears them talking.
Simon: I've never had a sister.
          Will you be my sis?
Grace: I've never had a brother.
          Will you be my bro?

So now they are Sis and Bro.
"I wish you'd get a Bro," Mom says to me.
Crazy lady!
The last thing I want
from my lovely, lovely Hal
is brotherly love.

drawing with light

Hal is passionate
about photography.
He disappears for hours into the bathroom
to develop his pictures,
emerging only when his brothers,
legs crossed,
are hammering on the door.

He tells Jinx,
"A famous photographer said
photography is 'drawing with light.'
That's what I'm trying to do."

Jinx looks at his pictures.
They are mainly of his family—
wonderful, intimate shots of
his brothers ducking under the hose,
his father in shorts and tank top,
hanging up the washing,
his mother, bald-headed, grinning
as she tosses her wig across the room.
And there is one of her, Jinx!
She's walking out of the subway,
out of darkness
into the light.

what we like about our moms

They jump out of bed at all hours to get you if you
    need a lift home.
They're much more patient than dads when you're
    learning to drive.
They're not too upset when you dent the bumper.
They understand that you simply *have* to have
    something new to wear to a party.
They're also more understanding about boyfriends
    than dads (who go out of their minds with rage
    imagining what boys might be up to).
They'll find the money somehow for an important
    school trip.
They organize holidays.
They believe guys should do half the housework.
They are nice to your friends.
They remember what it was like when all your
    friends have boyfriends and you don't.
They'll stay up all night to help out when the
    computer crashes and your essay is due first
    thing the next morning.
They give people a second chance.
They run a great taxi service.
They feed your pets.
They rearrange their lives to get to school functions.
They iron your clothes when you're running late.

They celebrate when you pass exams or get onto the
    sports team.
They commiserate when you don't.
They think you are the most
    wonderful/clever/beautiful person in the world,
    even if your only good feature is your eyebrows.
They forgive and forget.
They want the best for you.
They love you unconditionally.
They are always there when you need them.

JINX >>> longing

I long for Hal.
It's like a sickness.

When we're together
I wrap myself around him,
rub my cheek on the sleeve
of his jacket,
slip my hand under his shirt
to touch his heart.

We talk,
really talk.
He lets me into his head,
and I let him into mine.
I never knew it could be like this.

JINX >>> traveling

The Rat and Stella
want to check Hal out
so we have been invited to dinner.

Stella shows off
with such a battalion of cutlery
Grace gapes, awed.
Stella, pleased, instructs,
"Work from the outside in, dear."
As I sip
(pumpkin soup with a swirl of sour cream)
I start traveling—

I stroll along Hal's right eyebrow,
perch on the bridge of his nose,
trip through his eyelashes,
recline on his cheekbone,
get pleasantly lost
in the whorls of his ear,
slip between his lips,
slide down his chin,
and curl up
in the hollow of his throat.
I smile.
The Rat is thrilled,
thinking I'm laughing
at one of his jokes.

I try to catch Hal's eye,
then realize he is exploring *me*
so tenderly
I want to keep him nestled
in my throat
forever.

THE RAT >>> humming

I know she calls me the Rat.
It hurt.
But now I feel she says it with some affection,
as if I'm just a whiskery old fellow,
rather than a despised creature
slinking in the shadows.

Stella squeezes my hand under the table,
and I feel ridiculously happy—
here I am with my wife and daughters
and daughter's friend.
I want to burst into song,
but I sit quietly,
my heart humming.

JINX'S MOM >>> mystery

I saw a TV program
about an autistic woman,
very smart:
with lists
and training
and observation of others,
she is managing to lead
a nearly normal life.
But emotions remain a mystery
to her:
she will never love or hate,
feel sorrow, tenderness, or joy.
She cannot even bear to be touched,
except by a cumbersome machine
whose metallic, cushioned arms
hold her in an emotionless
loving embrace.

HAL >>> crazy about her

Little brothers are a curse—
especially when they hide
behind the sofa,
making kissing noises.
Jinx whispers,
"Let's do really disgusting
sucking sounds.
That'll gross them out."
It doesn't work.
The boys make even worse noises.
Jinx laughs,
and chases them out of the house
for a game of baseball.
They're crazy about her.
So am I.

reality tv

In disbelief,
Jinx's mom watches
a reality program
about a man who tries to cope
without his wife for a week.
Do some men really still think
it's cute
not to know how
to use an oven
or a washing machine,
never to have ironed a shirt,
or cleaned a toilet?
From what Jinx has told her,
Hal and his dad could show them
a thing or two.
Those guys can manage perfectly well
without a wife and mother.

Although Jinx's mom rarely prays,
she prays now that they will not have to.

JINX'S MOM >>> glorious

It doesn't happen very often,
so it was glorious to be in love,
(even if, *bugger*, it was unrequited).
The exhilaration,
the feeling of euphoria and hope
was worth the pain.

JINX >>> tangled

We take off our clothes
and lie down together.
He's ashamed of his body,
but he's as thin and beautiful
as my Etruscan man.
I tell him this
and he bops me with a pillow.
We wrestle
laughing,
our arms and legs tangled
like string.
He says quietly,
"I love you."

Suddenly
I'm so scared
I think my heart will stop.
He loves me.
I love him.

But I am Jinx.

JINX >>> the past

I can't stop myself—
I tell him about Charlie.
I tell him about Ben.

He's quiet for a long time.
He says,
"Someone wrote on the wall,
someone phoned at night.
My mother was ill, it made her afraid.
Was that you?"

I want to say no.
I want to wipe out the past.
I nod.

He stares at me,
his face thinner than ever.
He is crying
as softly, as silently
as the snow in the mountains.

He pulls on his clothes.
Runs from the house.

JINX >>> frozen

I lie in the dark
frozen as the Ping-Pong man.
Mom knocks on the door,
goes away,
knocks again.
"Jinx?"
The handle turns,
but the door is locked.
"Jinx! What's the matter?
Let me in, please. Jinx!"
I cannot move, cannot speak.
There's a soft tapping
at the door
and a small voice wailing,
"Jinx. I'm scared!"
Somehow I manage to crawl
out of bed,
creak across the room,
let Grace in.

JINX >>> pale sunshine

I put on my jacket
and walk to the bay.
Everywhere
are couples
or families
or single people exercising dogs.
Perhaps that's why they have dogs.
I walk fast,
as if I'm going somewhere,
hoping I won't bump into anyone I know.

Then I see her.
She's standing alone
by the water's edge,
her face radiant.

She turns,
puts her arm around my shoulders,
exclaims,
"Look how the water jumps with light.
It's like fish leaping!"

In the pale sunshine,
we stroll home together,
Mom and I.

JINX >>> tears

Grace looks wonderingly at me.
She says,
"Why're you crying?"
I stare at her.
"I'm not."
"Your evil eye is full of tears," says Grace.
I touch the bump on my forehead.
At last that damned pimple has surfaced.
"My evil eye has gone," I tell Grace.
"Forever?" she asks.
"Forever."

JINX >>> the first mark

From my window I see
terra-cotta chimney pots,
telephone lines railroading the sky,
and the suspension bridge
with its full-skirted cables.
Below,
the bay is wriggly with reflections,
home to black fish that spawn
once a year,
turning the water into a field of white flowers.

At night
the bridge is showy
with its hem of orange lights.
Police sirens swirl through the suburb,
provoking dogs to howl like wolves.
And windows of thin, wavy glass
rattle
as trucks shove through narrow streets.

I lay out paper, charcoal, pastels.
I take a deep breath,
pick up a great lump of charcoal,
and make the first mark.

JINX >>> thanks, mom

Mom doesn't ask why Hal
has vanished from my life.
She just says the two of us need
some "shopping therapy."
She hates shopping.
I drag her from store to store.
She buys a belt and a top,
but there's nothing I like.
Just as Mom's getting a wild,
hunted look in her eyes,
I choose a pair of walking boots.
In the holidays
I plan to explore my city—
north, south, east, and west.
I want to see bats flying over
the Botanical Gardens at dusk.
I want to see the sun rise at the
beach at Bondi.
I want to look at color and tone
and texture,
at light and dark,
at positive space,
at negative space.

I lace the boots firmly,
stand up,
take a step.

"Thanks, Mom," I say.
"For everything."

HAL >>> forgiveness

I wash the dishes,
Dad dries.
He looks tired.
Mom wakes three or four times a night.
We talk about a documentary we'd seen
about two small boys in Norway
who killed their playmate.
Though under supervision,
the boys are back with their families,
back at school.
"We don't jail *children*,"
explained a police officer.
I marvel at the generosity
of the murdered girl's mother,
at the forgiveness of the whole village.
Dad says,
"They will never forget such a terrible thing,
but if they do not forgive,
what hope is there for the boys, for any of them?"

JINX >>> starting again

For two weeks I don't see Hal
or hear from him.
I bury myself in work,
I tell only Ruthless what's happened.
One afternoon she makes me
go with her for coffee,
she says I need a break.
While she's waiting at the counter,
I take out my books,
might as well get a bit of studying done.
Suddenly I'm jostled,
water splashes down my neck, onto my books.
I swing around.
Hal smiles at me.
He says, "Shall we start again, Jinx?"
I smile back.
"Jen. My name's Jen."
"Hello, you," he says.

JEN >>> rainy afternoon

It's raining.
Mom is upstairs, reading.
Hal and Grace are playing cards.
I'm drawing them,
making lightning sketches,
trying to capture the moment.

It's raining.
Mom is making pancakes.
Hal and Grace and I are snuggled up
on the sofa,
watching *The Sound of Music*.
Hal has never seen it—
he doesn't know what he's in for!

JEN >>> last time

I dream of Charlie again.
Somehow I know it's for the last time.
He's standing at a crossroad,
but he doesn't seem lost.
He chooses a path,
strides away.
Then he turns and waves.